Home is where I can be me
and where you can be you.
Home is spending time together,
just us two.

When we go adventuring,
whether far or near,
home is where we come back to.
Home is always here.

Home is where we find
all the things we love the best.

Home is where we play.

Home is where we rest.

Home is safe and cosy.

When there is a storm . . .

outside it's wet and windy,

inside it's dry and warm.

Home's an extra special space
you hold within your heart,

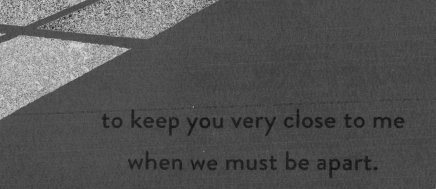

to keep you very close to me

when we must be apart.

It's more than just a building,
it's more than just a place.
Home is where you know that
you will see my smiling face.

So this I will remember
my whole life through.
Home is where the heart is . . .

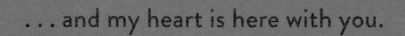

. . . and my heart is here with you.